# SCREAM STREET

## Book Six

## CLAW OF THE WEREWOLF

"Exactly the sort of grisly, gross,
and hilarious stuff that kids will love!"
Eoin Colfer

The fiendish fun continues at
www.screamstreet.com

# SCREAM STREET

## Book Six
## CLAW OF THE WEREWOLF

## TOMMY DONBAVAND

CANDLEWICK PRESS

Text copyright © 2009 by Tommy Donbavand
Illustrations copyright © 2009 by Cartoon Saloon Ltd.

First U.S. edition 2010

Library of Congress Cataloging-in-Publication Data

Donbavand, Tommy.
Claw of the werewolf / by Tommy Donbavand. —1st ed.
p.   cm. — (Scream Street ; 6)
Summary: With the sixth and final relic almost within his grasp,
Luke learns something unexpected about the author who has
been helping him in his quest to return with his terrified parents
to his own world, presenting a dilemma that is not helped by
a witch causing havoc in the neighborhood.
ISBN 978-0-7636-4638-7
[1. Horror stories. 2. Vampires—Fiction. 3. Mummies—Fiction.
4. Werewolves—Fiction. 5. Witches—Fiction.
6. Books and reading—Fiction.]   I. Title. II. Series.
PZ7.D7162Cl 2010
[Fic]—dc22       2010004398

10 11 12 13 14 15 16 SOL 10 9 8 7 6 5 4 3 2

Printed in Scott Junction, Quebec, Canada

This book was typeset in Bembo Educational.
The illustrations were done in ink.

Candlewick Press
99 Dover Street
Somerville, Massachusetts 02144

visit us at www.candlewick.com

For Kirsty, who opened the door for me

# Meet the residents

Luke Watson

Cleo Farr

Resus Negative

Dixon

Sir Otto Sneer

Samuel Skipstone

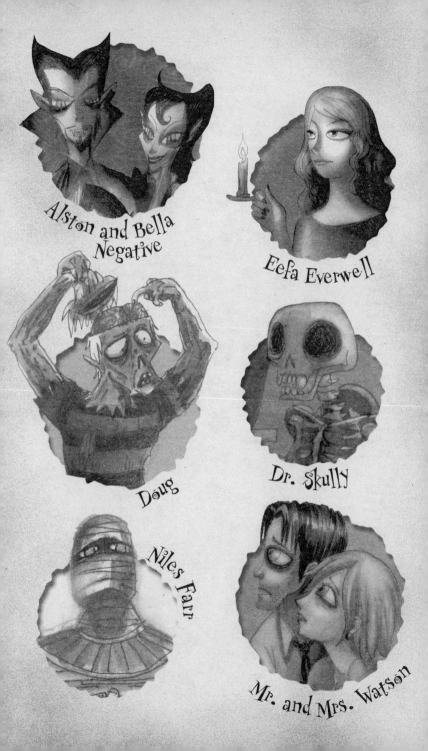

Alston and Bella Negative

Eefa Everwell

Doug

Dr. Skully

Niles Farr

Mr. and Mrs. Watson

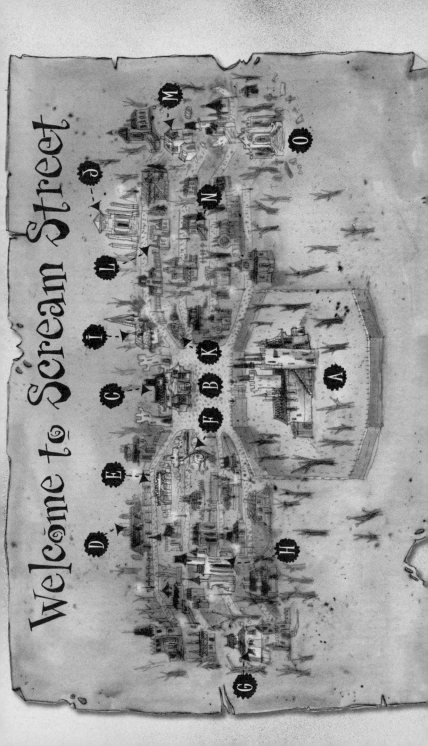

# Who lives where

# Previously on Scream Street . . .

Luke Watson was a perfectly ordinary boy until his tenth birthday, when he transformed into a werewolf. After it happened two more times, Luke and his family were forcibly moved by G.H.O.U.L. (Government Housing of Unusual Life-forms) to Scream Street, a community of ghosts, monsters, zombies, and more.

Luke quickly found his feet, making friends with Cleo Farr (a headstrong mummy) and Resus Negative, the son of the vampires next door. Luke soon realized, however, that Mr. and Mrs. Watson would never get over their fear of their nightmarish neighbors. With the help of an ancient book, *Skipstone's Tales of Scream Street,* Luke set out to find six relics, each left behind by one of the community's founding fathers. Only their combined power will enable him to open a doorway out of Scream Street and take his parents home.

Luke has just one relic left to locate, but in order to find it, he will have to learn a long-hidden secret about his family's past. . . .

# Chapter One
# The Witch

**With a creak** that echoed eerily around the deserted tomb, the golden sarcophagus swung open. The hieroglyphics covering its surface glinted in the light of the single flaming torch. A low moan sounded, and slowly, unsteadily, a figure wrapped from head to toe in bandages stumbled forward, arms outstretched. The mummy had been awakened.

*The two boys stood rooted to the spot as the mummy lurched into the middle of the tomb. Could the curse be true? Would they be forever hunted by this unstoppable creature, as the legend promised?*

*Suddenly, the mummy's head spun in their direction, black beetles squirming beneath the bandages that covered its decaying flesh. The boys stared in horror as it opened its mouth and screamed, sending a swarm of ravenous locusts toward them.*

*Within seconds, the boys were surrounded by the vile insects. They tried to run but were blinded by the thick, buzzing cloud. In their terror, the boys scrambled for the—*

Cleo Farr snapped the book closed and glared at the picture of the terrifying mummy on its cover. "That is *not* a children's book!" she exclaimed, tossing it onto the bed. "Mummies don't look anything like that, for a start."

A young vampire, Resus Negative, picked up the book. "*Bandages of Doom* by M. T. Graves," he read aloud, holding the cover up against Cleo's face. "I don't know," he said with a grin, "there's quite a resemblance there."

Cleo jumped indignantly to her feet and

2

smoothed down the bandages that covered her own body. *"One,"* she began, *"my* bandages are clean and ironed. *Two,* there are no beetles squirming around under them. And *three"*—Cleo opened her mouth wide to emphasize her point— "I have never screamed out a swarm of locusts in my life!"

"Calm down," said Resus. "It's just a book— and an old-fashioned one at that!"

Cleo glowered at her friend. "How would you like it if this M. T. Graves person wrote a book about *vampires* and got it all wrong?"

"He did," replied Resus, holding up another book, this one featuring a menacing vampire. *"Fangs of Destiny.* It's the next in the Horror Heights series." Resus laughed. "No vampire in the world would be seen undead in a cloak like that, and look—the shape of the fangs is all wrong!" He unclipped his own fangs as evidence.

"That doesn't mean anything," Cleo retorted. "They're not *real* vampire fangs!"

Resus bit back a reply. Born as a normal child to true vampire parents, he wore the fake fangs and white face paint along with dyeing his

hair black to help him look like the rest of his family. This deception, although accepted by all his friends, was still a touchy subject.

Cleo took the book from him and examined it. "Do kids really like reading this stuff?"

She and Resus turned to their friend Luke Watson for an answer—but none came. Luke had found the books while packing up his family's belongings, but now he sat staring at an old photo album, unaware of the conversation going on behind him.

"What's that?" Cleo asked.

*"The marriage of Michael Watson and Susan Skipton,"* said Resus, leaning over to read the golden lettering from the cover of the album. "Your mom and dad's wedding pictures!"

Luke nodded. "They looked so happy back then."

Luke's family had been moved to Scream Street after he had started transforming into a werewolf. From the very beginning his parents had been terrified of the street's unusual residents, and Luke couldn't remember the last time he had seen either of them smile.

Resus and Cleo had been helping him in his quest to find six relics left behind by Scream Street's founding fathers. Only when he had collected them all would he have the power to open a doorway back to his own world.

"They'll be happy again soon enough," Cleo said with a smile, sliding a golden casket from beneath Luke's bed. "Don't forget, there's only one relic left to find."

Luke placed the photo album back into its

 5

box. "That's why I want to get this packing finished. Once the doorway is open, I don't want to waste time racing around gathering up our belongings."

Resus flipped open the lid of the casket and examined the relics the trio had already located: a vial of witch's blood, a skeleton's skull, a mummy's heart, a zombie's tongue, and the fang of his own ancestor, Count Negatov. "It's quite a haul when you see it all together like this," he said, taking the fang and holding it up against the cover of *Fangs of Destiny*. "See," he added. "Completely the wrong shape!"

"Where did you get that?" demanded a voice.

Resus carefully replaced Count Negatov's fang and lifted out the silver copy of *Skipstone's Tales of Scream Street* that lay among the relics in the casket. The face on the cover of the book was scowling.

"It was tucked away behind the witch's blood," said Resus.

"I was not referring to the fang," replied the face. "I meant that book. It should not be here, in Scream Street!"

Luke took the metallic book from Resus and

 6

stood it up against the wall. "Why not?" he asked Samuel Skipstone, the owner of the face. "What's wrong with Horror Heights? I know they're old, but all the kids at my school loved them."

"They were never meant to leave your world," insisted Samuel Skipstone.

"So how do you know about them?"

Skipstone sighed. "I know—I mean, I *knew*—the author. He was a friend of mine."

"You knew M. T. Graves?" exclaimed Cleo. "Well, if you ever see him again . . ."

Skipstone forced a smile. "I rather think that in my current situation, further encounters with fellow scribes are unlikely, don't you?" The author had spent his natural life researching Scream Street, and at the time of his death he had cast a spell to merge his spirit with the pages of his book so that he could continue his work.

Luke grabbed the Horror Heights books and added them to the pile in the box. "Well, soon I'll be taking them out of Scream Street forever."

"Forever?" whispered Cleo. "You'll never be back?"

"I'm trying not to think about it," Luke said, sighing.

 7

"Is that right, Mr. Skipstone?" Cleo asked the author. "Once Luke leaves Scream Street, can he never come back?"

"I am afraid not," replied the silver face. "The doorway to Luke's world will remain open only long enough for his wish to be fulfilled. Once he and his family have passed through, it will close behind them for all time."

Cleo looked at Luke, her eyes filling with tears. "I'll miss you."

"Good grief!" groaned Resus. "We'll both miss him, blubber bandages, but there's no need to get all sappy about it." He pulled a handkerchief from his cloak and handed it to her. As he did so, something clattered to the floor: a small dog's collar. "I'd forgotten I had that," said the vampire as Luke bent to pick it up.

Luke studied the silver name tag. It was encrusted with dried blood, and a smudge of marker pen obscured the first letter of the name, Fluffy. "This was what the chihuahua was wearing."

"Chihuahua?" asked Cleo.

"The dog that bit me—bit my werewolf— when it attacked a bully from my old school."

Luke shuddered as he recalled the moment when he had been about to pounce on the bully and the tiny dog had nipped his ankle. His werewolf had turned to chase after the chihuahua and the bully had escaped, scared but unharmed.

"There's blood on the collar," said Cleo. "You didn't . . ."

Luke shook his head. "I grabbed the dog by the ear with my teeth, but it wriggled out of its collar and ran off. If it hadn't stopped me, though . . ."

"But it *did* stop you," Resus pointed out. "The bully got away. The only thing to happen was for you to be moved here—and you can't say that life in Scream Street has been *all* bad."

"It's had its moments," admitted Luke, managing a smile.

Samuel Skipstone gave a polite cough from the cover of his book. "You are discussing young Master Watson's departure as though it were happening this minute," he said. "May I remind you that there is another relic to locate first?"

"You're right," said Luke, pushing the boxes aside. "I've had enough of packing. Let's start looking!"

The trio gathered around *Skipstone's Tales of*

*Scream Street,* and the book flicked through its handwritten pages, finally stopping at a pantomime script: *Sleeping Ugly.* Before their eyes, the lines of dialogue and stage directions began to fade away to reveal the clue to the location of the final relic.

Suddenly there was a bright orange flash behind them and a witch appeared on top of Luke's box of books, wearing crumpled red-and-yellow robes and clutching a large black sack. Realizing that her hair was on fire, she calmly patted out the flames and beamed at the gaping trio.

"Tress Wunder," she announced. "Now, where do you want this order of quill boxes?"

# Chapter Two
# The Water

**Luke, Resus, and Cleo** stared at the witch in stunned silence.

"This *is* Everwell's Emporium, isn't it?" she asked, climbing out of the box, the ends of her hair still smoldering.

"Ah," said Cleo, light dawning. "No, I'm afraid you're a few streets out."

"You make stuff for Everwell's?" Resus asked the witch.

"Indeed I do," she replied, producing from the sack a small silver box with a carving of a feather quill on the top.

"That's lovely," said Cleo, admiring it. "What is it for?"

The witch looked blank and stared down at the box as though seeing it for the first time. "Do you know, I've absolutely no idea."

"Still, it's nice," Cleo assured her. "Eefa told us she was getting some new stuff in."

"Did she?" asked Luke.

"Yes," replied Cleo. "Yesterday, when we were collecting the empty boxes so you could start packing."

Luke shook his head, puzzled. "Nope, don't remember that at all."

"Me neither," agreed Resus.

Cleo grunted in frustration. "Boys!"

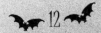

12

"Now, now," said Tress. "Being, indeed, mere boys, they were probably thrown by Miss Everwell's enchantment charm."

Cleo shrugged, suspecting she was right. All witches had the ability to look stunningly beautiful, and it wouldn't be the first time that Luke and Resus had fallen under Eefa's spell.

Tress swept her greasy hair over her shoulder and ran a broken fingernail over her pockmarked cheek. "I myself have been known to turn heads around the world," she added.

Resus stared. "Probably because they didn't want you to see them throwing up!" he exclaimed before he could stop himself. He howled as Cleo kicked him in the shin.

"What do you mean by that?" demanded Tress, darting across the room to look at herself in the mirror. She gasped at her reflection. "Oh, dear!" she cried. "My charm must have worn off during the journey!" She clicked her fingers and a faint orange light fizzed around her once more.

When the witch turned back, she had transformed into a vision of pure beauty. Thick red hair fell in long, wavy tresses over her shoulders, her pale skin was as smooth as porcelain and her

 13

lips were colored a vibrant crimson. Resus and Luke stared in astonishment, their mouths hanging open.

"Now," Tress cooed, flicking a strand of hair out of her eyes with a long red fingernail. "Who can show me the way to Everwell's Emporium?"

The relic immediately forgotten, Luke and Resus both blubbed something unintelligible and launched for the door. Resus caught his foot in his cape and tripped, pulling Luke down with him.

Cleo rolled her eyes as she stepped over the boys and out onto the landing. "I will," she said.

Cleo led Tress Wunder along Scream Street toward the central square while Luke and Resus stumbled along behind carrying the sack of heavy silver boxes between them.

The witch was surprised to see that many of the houses had broken windows, smashed doors, and damaged fences. Residents were busy repairing what they could with the few materials available.

"What happened here?" she asked.

"We had a visit from a demon," Cleo told her. "He destroyed a couple of houses completely; the rest of us got away with just a few broken windows."

"But surely you have Movers here," said the witch. "Shouldn't they be out fixing things?"

Luke felt a chill run down his spine at the mention of the faceless men who had relocated his family to Scream Street after the incident with the school bully. "Our landlord says they can't start work repairing the street until they've finished some jobs for him," he explained.

The group entered the central square to see several dozen Movers busy at work on Sneer Hall, the ancestral home of Scream Street's land-lord, Sir Otto Sneer. The rampaging demon had demolished the walls in several places, and the Movers were hastily patching them up.

"He's got the Movers working on his own home?" cried Tress in disgust. "What a selfish toad! He should be putting his residents first."

"Sir Otto doesn't quite think that way," began Resus.

"Then allow me to put him right!" said Tress, clicking her fingers. There was a flash, and Sir Otto Sneer suddenly appeared in the square beside them, chewing on a fat cigar.

 15

"What the—" he grunted. "Which of you freaks dragged me out here?"

"I did," said Tress firmly. "I must insist that you stop repairs on your own home and send the Movers out to work on your residents' houses. Immediately!"

Sir Otto pushed his face up close to the witch's. "And what if I say no?"

"Then I shall be very, very angry."

Sir Otto blew a cloud of smoke into her face and laughed. "Shove off, freak!" he snarled.

"Your pathetic enchantment spell won't work on me."

Without a moment's pause, Tress whipped her hand around and slapped Sir Otto hard in the face. Luke, Resus, and Cleo winced as the landlord's cigar flew out of his mouth.

"You'll regret that!" Sir Otto growled, his eyes blazing with anger. And pulling a fresh cigar from his jacket pocket, he jammed it into his mouth and strode away.

"Well!" exclaimed Tress as they watched him go. "I have never met such a rude and insolent man in my life."

"You should visit more often," said Luke. "He does a pretty good 'obnoxious' and 'mean,' too."

"And *these* are disgusting," added the witch, collecting up the discarded cigar.

"They're just part of his charm," said Resus. "It was Sir Otto who let the demon loose on Scream Street, you know."

"*What?* This behavior should not be tolerated," insisted Tress. "I shall talk to Miss Everwell about this!" And she turned on her heel and marched toward the emporium.

"Does anyone else have the feeling this won't

end well?" said Cleo. "I think we'd better follow her."

The bat perched above the doorway of Everwell's Emporium screeched as Luke, Resus, and Cleo all trooped inside. They arrived just in time to see Eefa drop Sir Otto's cigar into a bubbling cauldron as Tress looked on, giggling.

The trio rushed over to the witches. "Sorry to intrude," said Resus quickly, "but can I ask what you beautiful ladies are up to?"

Eefa Everwell, looking as stunning as ever in a slinky purple dress, smiled as she added a little water to the cauldron from a nearby bucket. The landlord's cigar slowly sank beneath the surface of the shimmering liquid. "Tress told me how Sir Otto spoke to her," she said. "We're making certain he never does it again."

Cleo paled beneath her bandages. "You're not going to . . ."

"Of course not," Tress laughed. "We're witches, not murderers!" She grabbed a handful of squirming maggots from a jar on the shop counter and dropped them into the cauldron. They were met with a bubble and a hiss.

"So what *are* you doing?" asked Luke.

"Well," said Eefa as she stirred the mixture, "let's just say that Sir Otto's latest cigar is about to change into something slightly more disgusting."

"Want to see?" Tress asked mischievously. She snapped her fingers, and in another flash of light, Sir Otto appeared in the emporium, sucking on a squirming black leech.

The landlord shrieked and spat the creature out, frantically rubbing the slime from his tongue. Hearing laughter, he looked up and realized where he was.

"You!" he growled at the sight of Tress. "I'll teach you a lesson you'll never forget!" And with that, he grabbed the bucket of water from beside the counter and threw it over her.

Tress Wunder screamed.

# Chapter Three
## The Flu

"**What have you done?**" spluttered Tress, drenched from head to toe.

Sir Otto Sneer's mouth twisted into a wide grin. "I know my folklore," he said. "Witches are allergic to water! I can't wait for you to start melting."

"*Melting?*" demanded Eefa. "That's ridiculous! If we were allergic to water, we'd shrivel up in the shower every morning."

The landlord looked confused. "Then why were you screaming?" he asked Tress.

"Because I've been fighting off the flu for the past two weeks!" wailed the witch, wringing water from her sodden dress. "Now I'll be drinking hot tea every night until . . . until . . . unt—ACHOO!"

As Tress's sneeze echoed around the shop, the bat above the door was suddenly bathed in a burst of orange light. When the flash subsided, the bat had turned into a goat. The creature clung onto the perch with its hooves and bleated in terror.

"What was *that*?" asked Cleo.

Before anyone could reply, Tress sneezed again. "ACHOO!" This time the cauldron flashed briefly before transforming into a model ship.

Again and again, Tress sneezed. All around the shop, objects flashed into new shapes. "ACHOO!" Eefa's cash register became a two-headed sheep. "ACHOO!" Luke's watch changed into a glittering butterfly. And the jar of maggots on the counter was suddenly—"ACHOO!"—a crystal bowling ball.

"What's going on?" asked Luke, only just catching the goat as it fell from its perch above the door. He set the animal down and it ran into a corner, where it stood and trembled.

"It's the real reason witches don't like cold water!" Eefa shouted above Tress's sneezes. "Witch flu can have disastrous consequences!"

"Can you change these things back?" asked Resus, jumping to one side as the goat scurried past, trying to escape a huge toad that was the result of another giant sneeze.

"ACHOO!"

Eefa nodded. "I should be able to put everything right," she promised. "What's important now is to get Tress to bed, where she can get better and stop sneezing out magic." She grabbed her robes from the coatrack just before it transformed into a baby giraffe, and wrapped them around her friend.

"You freaks are all as bad as each other!" bellowed Sir Otto, yanking the shop door open and marching outside. "I'm going somewhere sane!"

"Will Tress be OK?" asked Cleo as the door closed behind the landlord.

"I'll mix her up a potion," said Eefa. "That will help her, although it might be a while before she starts to feel better. The good news, however, is that her sneezes will affect only the emporium, as this is the only place she's been to today."

"Aside from Luke's house, that is," said Resus.

"ACHOO!"

"She's been to Luke's house?" asked Eefa. "Oh, dear!"

"I don't like the sound of that 'oh, dear,'" said Luke.

"If Tress flashed into your house before coming here, there's a possibility that she'll have left some of her magical residue there," explained the witch.

"Magical residue?" asked Cleo.

"It's like a witch's fingerprint," explained Eefa. "It follows her wherever she goes."

"What's so bad about that?" asked Resus.

"When a witch has the flu, her sneezes can affect anything touched by her magical residue that day, including—"

"ACHOO!"

"My bedroom," groaned Luke. "Why do these things always happen to my house?" With a heavy sigh, he pulled open the shop door and raced out across the square, Resus and Cleo at his heels.

The bleating goat tried to follow them, but as the result of another sneeze—"ACHOO!"—it changed into a giant cabbage and sat perfectly still.

The trio ran through the front door to 13 Scream Street just as it—"ACHOO!"—flashed and began to turn into a ring of flowers. Inside, objects were transforming faster and faster. "ACHOO!" An oil painting became an owl and batted its wings against the wall for a moment before flapping to freedom through an open window.

"Tress's cold must be getting worse," said Resus as—"ACHOO!"—a vase of flowers on the table in the hallway became a lump of lemon Jell-O and fell to the floor with a *splat*!

"How come we can still hear her sneezes?" demanded Cleo.

Resus shrugged. "I guess they're tied in with the magic."

"Mom? Dad? Where are you?" shouted Luke.

"ACHOO!" Above him, a burst of light erupted across the ceiling. Cleo dragged him to one side just as the chandelier transformed into an anvil and smashed to the floor.

"We're in here!"

Luke raced toward the living room at the sound of his dad's voice. Running in, he was temporarily blinded by an orange flash that—"ACHOO!"—enveloped the sofa on which his parents were huddled. A split-second later, they were both sitting on the back of a gymnastic vaulting horse. The coffee table beside it—"ACHOO!"—zapped itself into a bottle of champagne.

"Are you OK?" Luke asked.

"We're fine!" called Mr. Watson, dragging his wife off the vaulting horse and kicking it to the other side of the room, just as—"ACHOO!"—it became a wild boar. "We only just got back; the zombies needed some help with their plumbing."

Luke stared at his dad, stunned. "You've been around to the zombies' house to fix the plumbing?"

"ACHOO!" The bottle of champagne turned into a large rat.

"Don't be so surprised," said his mom. "Your dad's always been good with things like that." The rat scuttled up her leg, and she grabbed it by the tail and hurled it through the open window. "Horrible creatures!"

Luke was lost for words. Could these be the same parents who, just weeks ago, had been terrified by anything to do with Scream Street? "Resus," he said, finally finding his voice, "take my mom and dad to your house."

"Why?" asked Mr. Watson. "Is their plumbing acting up too?"

"No, it's just that—"

Just then, the wallpaper—"ACHOO!"—flashed into millions of terrified cockroaches, which immediately scuttled for cover, causing the walls to look as though they were rippling.

Resus screamed in terror.

Luke shook his head. This was all the wrong way around! "Mom, Dad, take Resus home!" he called. "I'll explain later, but this is only happening here. Cleo will go with you."

"What about you?" asked his dad as— "ACHOO!"—the armchair became a rather nervous sheep.

"I need to check something upstairs, then I'll join you."

Giving him a quick thumbs-up, Mr. and Mrs. Watson grabbed Resus and pulled him from the room. As Luke and Cleo made to follow, the screeching boar spotted the sheep and charged at it. The sheep leaped aside, causing the boar to smash into a wooden bookcase, which crashed to the floor, scattering books everywhere.

"Look out!" called Luke before jumping over the books and heading for the stairs to rescue

*Skipstone's Tales of Scream Street* and the casket of relics before something happened to them. Then he stopped, realizing that Cleo was no longer with him. He turned to find her trapped beneath the bookcase.

"Can't . . . move," she grunted. "Think my arm . . . might be . . . broken!"

Luke dropped quickly to his knees and pushed frantically at the bookcase, trying to slide it off his friend. It moved slightly, but Cleo screamed as a lightning bolt of pain shot down her injured arm.

"You have to . . . lift it," she hissed through gritted teeth. "Don't . . . slide it again."

"I can't!" cried Luke. "It's too heavy!"

"Please," begged Cleo, blinking back tears of pain.

Luke glared angrily at the bookcase, and a wave of darkness flushed through his body. This was the rage that would allow him to change into his werewolf form. Since he'd moved to Scream Street, he had been learning how to direct the transformation to a particular area of his body. He needed that power more than ever now.

Forcing the anger down through his arms, he watched as rapidly developing muscles pressed

 29

against the thin fabric of his shirt. Bones stretched as his fingers became long claws, and his entire upper body sprouted coarse brown fur.

Luke grabbed the heavy bookcase and lifted it a few inches off the floor. His whole body trembled with the effort, but the gap was wide enough for Cleo to slide through.

As Luke dropped the bookcase back to the floor, the mummy climbed shakily to her feet, her broken arm hanging limply at her side.

"That's a weight off," she quipped before collapsing into a dead faint.

# Chapter Four
# The Body

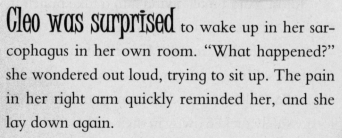

**Cleo was surprised** to wake up in her sarcophagus in her own room. "What happened?"
she wondered out loud, trying to sit up. The pain
in her right arm quickly reminded her, and she
lay down again.

Luke appeared beside the bed. "Your arm's
broken in two places," he said. "Your dad dipped
some fresh bandages into a paste he made out of

lotus flowers and set it for you." Cleo lifted the heavy cast to examine it.

"What happened to the wild boar?" she asked.

"Getting used to life as a sofa again!" said Resus, entering the room.

"Has everything been changed back?" asked Luke.

"Eefa's at your house now," replied Resus, "busy sorting it all out. It looks like Tress's flu is getting a little better, too: the only thing I saw change while I was there was the kitchen stove—into a rather confused-looking badger."

"What about Mr. Skipstone?"

"He looks nothing like a confused badger," said the vampire, grinning.

"Idiot!" said Luke, giving him a fake punch in the arm. "I *mean,* did you get the book?"

"Right here," replied his friend, producing *Skipstone's Tales of Scream Street* from under his cloak. "You'll be pleased to know that all the relics are safely tucked away in their casket and none of them has been zapped into a new identity."

"Good," said Luke, relieved. "It looks like my mom and dad will be out of here soon."

"So will you," Cleo reminded him as he took the silver book from Resus. "But is leaving Scream Street what you want?"

Luke's cheeks flushed as he struggled for an answer. "I . . . that is . . . I just want my mom and dad to get their old lives back!" he said eventually, turning away as Resus and Cleo exchanged a glance.

"If you want to stay, you should say so," said Cleo gently.

"I *don't* want to, OK?" snapped Luke. "I want things to be back the way they were — with my old house, my old school . . . and my old mom and dad back!" He flicked through *Skipstone's Tales of Scream Street* to the pantomime script. "Give us the clue to the final relic, please, Mr. Skipstone."

"Luke, I think —" began Resus.

"The final clue, please, Mr. Skipstone!" Luke repeated more loudly.

With a sigh, the author began to fade the pantomime scene where Prince Luckless slips a paper bag over Sleeping Ugly's head before kissing her. Hidden beneath was the clue to the last founding father's relic:

> Listen close and hear my rhyme.
> The house you seek is at its prime.
> The task at hand will shock the meek,
> for now a werewolf's claw you seek.

Luke took a deep breath. "A werewolf's claw," he whispered. "Other werewolves have lived in Scream Street!"

"It must have been ages ago," said Resus. "When you first moved in, my mom and dad said they couldn't remember ever having had a werewolf for a neighbor."

"Where's the relic hidden, though?" asked Cleo. "I don't understand the clue at all. *The house you seek is at its prime.* What does that mean?"

"I don't know," admitted Luke, closing the book. "Maybe we have to go to whichever house in Scream Street is the nicest or best decorated. That's what 'at its prime' means, isn't it?"

"It can't be that," said Resus. "How would the founding father know what the houses would look like when someone eventually found his clue?"

"Do you know what it means, Mr. Skipstone?" Cleo asked the silver book. The face on the cover

34

remained silent, its eyes closed.

"Mr Skipstone?" said Luke. The book didn't reply.

"Was it something I said?" asked Cleo.

Luke shook his head. "I'm beginning to understand how it works. Mr. Skipstone will only help us so far, then the rest is up to us."

"We haven't done too badly until now," Cleo reminded him with a smile.

"That's true," said Luke, tucking *Skipstone's Tales of Scream Street* into the back pocket of his jeans and standing up, "but we won't find out anything sitting here. Come on, Resus."

Cleo leaped out of her sarcophagus. "What do you mean, 'Come on, Resus'?" she demanded. "What about me?"

"You can't come," said Luke. "You've got a broken arm!"

"And how does that stop me?"

"You need to rest," he replied.

Cleo squared up to him, her eyes flaring. "Luke Watson," she said slowly, "I have helped you to find five out of the six founding fathers' relics. If you try to leave me out of the hunt for the last one, I'll show you just how hard these

 35

lotus-flower-plaster casts can be."

Luke couldn't help but smile. "I wouldn't dream of leaving you out," he protested, holding up his arms to defend himself. "After you!"

Sticking her tongue out at him, Cleo led the way down the stairs. As she reached the bottom, she called into the kitchen, "Dad, I'm going out with Luke and Resus."

A tall Egyptian mummy, Niles Farr, appeared in the hallway, a tea towel in his hands. "But your arm needs—"

"My arm feels fine," insisted Cleo. "Besides, if I get into any trouble, I've got these two ugly mugs to look after me."

Niles Farr bowed solemnly to Luke and Resus. "Your friendship with my daughter humbles me," he pronounced.

Cleo blushed. "Dad!"

"Allow me to finish," insisted Niles. "When we left our pyramid, many moons ago, our prime reason was for Cleo to find such friendship as this."

"Dad, I mean it—"

"What did you say?" interrupted Resus. "Your *prime* reason?"

Cleo's father nodded solemnly. "It was first and foremost in my mind. She would have been alone had we remained where we were."

"Come on," said Cleo, practically dragging the boys toward the front door. "He'll go on all day if you let him. Bye, Dad!"

"Your dad's *prime reason*," Luke said thoughtfully as the trio stepped out into the street. "The reason that was first and foremost in his mind when you left Egypt . . ."

"Which means," finished Resus, "that *prime* can also mean *first.*"

"So, if we're looking for a house that's *at its prime*," said Cleo, catching on, "we need the first house."

Luke grinned. "The final relic must be hidden at number one Scream Street!"

The inside of 1 Scream Street was dark and dusty, and Luke opened the living-room curtains to provide a little light. The children had knocked but received no reply, so they'd decided to explore the house uninvited. A locked front door had proved to be no obstacle for Resus's fake vampire talons.

"Whoever lives here obviously doesn't believe in cleaning up," said Cleo as she picked her way through piles of books and letters on the floor. Every surface, from the sofa to the windowsill, was stacked high with some sort of reading material.

"I don't think anyone can live here anymore," said Resus, picking up an old copy of *The Terror Times* and blowing dust from it.

"Maybe we've got it wrong," said Cleo, puzzled. "I can't imagine a werewolf living—"

"*Shh,*" interrupted Luke, pointing. "There's someone there!" Resus and Cleo followed his gaze across the hallway to the study, where they spotted a figure sitting in an ancient swivel chair at a long desk, its back to the trio.

Resus cleared his throat. "Excuse me," he called out. The figure didn't respond, and the vampire gestured for his friends to follow him. As they got closer, the trio could see that the desk was covered in pages of handwritten manuscript and old-fashioned quills. A bottle of ink, a quill still dipped in it, sat beside the papers.

"We're sorry to burst in," Cleo began politely. "We did knock." The figure remained motionless

and silent. "Why doesn't he answer?" she hissed to the others.

"I don't think he *can* answer," said Luke. "I think he might be dead." Cleo's eyes widened, and she gave a whimper.

"What's wrong with you?" demanded Resus. "You live in a street surrounded by skeletons and zombies, and you're worried about being in the same room as a corpse!" He tapped the figure on the shoulder. "See? Dead as a dodo."

"Stop it," ordered Cleo.

"Why?" Resus asked with a grin. "He doesn't mind—do you?" He grabbed one of the dead body's hands and waved it at the mummy.

"I said, stop it!" shouted Cleo, slapping the hand from Resus's grasp.

The momentum caused the chair to spin around so that the figure was facing the trio. They froze, looks of terror on their faces. Although the skin was pulled paper thin across the bones, the face was easy to identify.

Sitting in the chair was the lifeless body of Samuel Skipstone.

# Chapter Five

# The Werewolf

"**I don't get it,**" said Luke, staring in amazement at the dried-up figure. A jacket, shirt, and tie hung limply from its shrunken frame. "This is supposed to be where the last founding father lives. What's Mr. Skipstone doing here?"

"Not much, by the look of it," said Resus, giving the corpse an experimental nudge. It swayed slightly in its chair.

Cleo was unable to tear her eyes away. "It's horrible!"

Luke pulled *Skipstone's Tales of Scream Street* from his pocket. "What's going on here?" he asked the silver face.

"You have found my body exactly where I left it when my spirit merged with this book," replied Samuel Skipstone. His eyes flickered around the room. "No one will have been inside this house since."

"Then how did the book get out?" said Resus. "And wouldn't G.H.O.U.L. have needed the house for another family?"

"A close friend was with me when I cast the spell," explained Skipstone. "Femur Ribs."

"The skeleton who gave Luke her skull as a relic?" asked Cleo.

"The same," said Skipstone. "She took the book with her and spread a rumor that ownership of the house had passed on to my son."

"Your *son*?" asked Luke. "You had a family?"

"I still do," said the author with a smile.

"But you did live here, with the last founding father?" said Luke.

"Not exactly . . ." began Skipstone.

"Then you must have allowed him to hide the final relic here."

Skipstone's silver eyes looked intently up at Luke from the cover of his book. "Luke," he said patiently, "I *am* the last founding father."

Luke felt his head swim at the news, and he was forced to clutch the edge of the desk. "You can't be," he gasped. "The last founding father was a werewolf!"

"You are correct," agreed the face on the book. "I was—*am*—a werewolf, just like you. And just like you I struggled to control my transformations whenever I grew angry, and was occasionally a threat to the people I loved." The author sighed heavily. "Finally leaving my body was something of a relief. But now I must return."

"Return?" exclaimed Resus, staring at what was left of the corpse. "Into *that*?"

"It has to be done," said Skipstone. "I must leave behind my life's work and transform one last time. That is why my body was not buried."

"Wait," said Cleo, her voice trembling. "You once said you had transferred your spirit to the book as you were dying. That's right, isn't it?"

 43

"I don't think I want to hear this . . ." began Luke.

"Hear it or not, it remains the truth," said Skipstone firmly. "When the spell is reversed, I shall return to my body as it was, on the verge of death."

"That's OK," Luke said thoughtfully. "We can just put you back in the book once I have the claw."

"I fear that will not be possible," replied the author. "Once I leave this book, it will be destroyed. I shall die."

"Then we'll find another one!" insisted Luke.

Skipstone sighed. "*Tales of Scream Street* was my only book."

"That's ridiculous!" cried Luke. "You're an author! There's no way you wrote only one book." And dashing across the room to a creaking bookshelf, he began to pull out book after book, checking the covers for Samuel Skipstone's name.

Resus sighed. "Luke, we understand that you're upset. . . ."

"No!" snapped Luke, flinging more and more volumes to the floor. "You *don't* understand,

Resus. All I wanted to do was take my mom and dad home—and now, after all we've been through, I find out I have to kill someone in order to do it!"

"You would not be killing me, Luke," Skipstone interrupted. "I cheated death to begin with by becoming part of this book. All we would be doing is putting everything back to rights."

"Won't you just become a zombie, Mr. Skipstone, like Doug or Berry?" asked Cleo.

"Sadly, no," replied the author. "For that process to occur, a body must be buried and rise from its grave soon afterward. I was never buried—and I fear it would be too late to do so now."

"So, we're just supposed to be happy that you're about to croak?" snapped Luke, yanking open the top drawer of an antique filing cabinet and beginning to rifle through it.

"No one is happy about it, Luke," said Skipstone. "I always knew this would happen one day—that I would assist someone in finding the relics and then return to my body to die. I am just pleased it was *you* I was able to help."

Luke shook his head. "It can't happen like that—there *has* to be a way we can—"

He stopped, pulling a handwritten manuscript from the back of the drawer. "Here we go!" he announced triumphantly. "I'd know this handwriting anywhere."

"Luke, don't—" began Skipstone.

"Once I've got your claw," said Luke excitedly, waving the manuscript, "we can use the spell to put you in *this,* and you can live on!"

"Please—"

"I know it hasn't got a cover yet," Luke added, "but once your spirit is in the pages, we can make one and it'll look just like a real book."

"I really don't think—"

Luke continued to ignore the author. "It might not be as grand as *Skipstone's Tales of Scream Street*," he said, flipping over the first page of the manuscript, "but I'm sure you'll soon get used to being—"

He stopped when he saw the title, then slowly he read aloud: "*Bandages of Doom* by M. T. Graves." The room fell silent.

Cleo was the first to speak. "*You're* M. T. Graves?" she asked. "You wrote those kids' books about mummies and vampires?"

"They were my first published books,"

46

Skipstone admitted awkwardly. "I wrote them when I lived in Luke's world, before the Movers brought me to Scream Street. Before I knew what vampires and mummies were really like."

"Why 'M. T. Graves'?" asked Resus. "Why not use your real name?"

"G.H.O.U.L. was after me," explained the author. "We Skipstones were known to be were-wolves. I couldn't let them track me down, or I'd end up . . ."

"Here," Luke finished, still marveling to think that Samuel Skipstone came from Luke's own world.

"Exactly," said Skipstone. "After he got married, my son even dropped a few letters from our last name in an effort to throw G.H.O.U.L. off the scent."

"How did they find you in the end?" asked Resus.

"Some other authors made fun of my books," replied Skipstone. "They said that what I was writing was ridiculous. It made me so angry, I transformed and destroyed half of my local library."

"I can see how that might have attracted G.H.O.U.L.'s attention!" Cleo said, grinning.

"So, you and your son were brought to Scream Street. . . ."

Skipstone shook his silvery head. "Just me," he said. "I wouldn't tell them where to find my wife and son, and mercifully they remained free. I never saw them again," he added sadly.

"Well, you'll be seeing *us* again," said Luke. "Once I've got the final relic I can save you in this M. T. Graves manuscript."

"Are you sure it will work?" asked Cleo.

"Technically, there is no reason why it would not," said Skipstone, a hopeful tone creeping into his voice. "The spell should still be active both ways after all these years."

"Then what are we waiting for?" said Luke, beaming. "What's the spell?"

"You should find it on the desk," said Skipstone. "It was the last thing I wrote. Place the book near my body, then write out the spell in reverse. It will only work if the words are written down."

Resus found a folded piece of paper by the author's quill and, unfolding it, read out the words written there:

Rats live on no evil star

"*Rats live on no evil star?*" repeated Cleo. "What does that mean?"

"Probably nothing," said Resus. "It's just words that make up a spell."

"OK," said Luke, laying *Skipstone's Tales of Scream Street* on the floor in front of the body and pulling a pencil from his pocket. "Let's write it backward." Grabbing a nearby piece of paper, he began to copy out the sentence in reverse. "*R-a-t-s-l-i*—" He stopped. "The spell reads the same backward as it does forward! *Rats live on no evil star!*"

The face on the cover of the silver book smiled. "To realize the power of word—that is the true magic!"

As Luke finished writing, a shimmering light rose up from *Skipstone's Tales of Scream Street*, flickering like a flame. It hovered there for a moment and then slipped into the mouth of the dead body and disappeared.

With a gasp, the decayed body of Samuel Skipstone opened its eyes and blinked. "Did it work?" he asked hoarsely. "Am I back?"

Luke smiled. "You are!"

**Samuel Skipstone** pushed his hands against the sides of his chair and tried to stand, but the effort was too great and he collapsed down again, coughing.

"Are you OK?" asked Cleo.

Skipstone nodded slowly. "These old muscles have wasted considerably," he said. "There is not much movement left in them, I fear."

"Look at the book!" exclaimed Resus. They all turned to see *Skipstone's Tales of Scream Street*, its cover now a plain expanse of silver, shudder slightly, then suddenly dissolve into a pile of ash on the floor.

"My life's work—gone!" The author gave a weak smile. "I guess that having me as a lodger must have been quite a burden for it," he said.

"It was a wonderful book, Mr. Skipstone," said Luke. "It helped me to find the relics I need to take my parents away from Scream Street."

"Not all of them," Resus reminded him. "You still need the werewolf's claw."

"And for that, I shall have to transform," said Skipstone, coughing again. "I am unpracticed at controlling my transformations, however, so it might take a while for my hands to change."

Cleo put her arm around the frail old man. "Are you sure you can manage it?"

Before Skipstone could reply, Luke had snatched up the bottle of ink from the desk, pulled out the stopper, and poured it over the carpet.

"What did you do that for?" asked Skipstone.

"To make you angry," said Luke. "To make you transform!"

Skipstone shrugged feebly. "That won't do it. I never liked this carpet."

Luke grunted in frustration. "Come on," he said to Resus. "Help me!"

"OK," said the vampire. "Er . . . *Skipstone's Tales of Scream Street* was full of utter nonsense."

"What better place to hide the clues to the founding fathers' relics?"

"This is ridiculous," snapped Luke. "There must be something that will make you as angry as that bad review did!" A smile spread across his face as a thought occurred. "Cleo hated *Bandages of Doom*, you know."

Skipstone's expression darkened. "What?"

"Luke, what are you doing?" exclaimed Cleo.

"It's true," agreed Resus, catching on. "She said that mummies would never behave that way, and that the curse you wrote in it was like baby talk."

Skipstone spun his chair around to glare at Cleo.

"I really don't think this is a good idea. . . ." she began.

"In fact," continued Luke, "she said that

52

Horror Heights was the worst series of children's books she had ever read!"

He gave a deep-throated growl, and then Samuel Skipstone's eyes flashed red and he began to transform into a werewolf. His decomposed skin sprouted with silver fur, and his shriveled muscles swelled.

"Er, I don't think this is going to be a partial transformation, guys," warned Resus. "This looks like the full thing to me!"

Its powerful teeth gnashing, the wolf leaped from its chair, straight for Cleo. As the mummy dived under the desk, the old wolf snapped at her ankles, and she could feel its hot breath on her bandages. She screamed.

"Mr. Skipstone!" roared Luke, grabbing the chair and swinging it around, catching the werewolf in the side of its head and knocking it off balance. "Don't do this!" The silver wolf shook its head to clear the blow and spun to face him.

Gripped by terror, Luke stood rooted to the spot as Skipstone's wolf gave a roar and lunged for him, fangs bared—only to find a flame thrust in front of its snout.

"Good thing I had one of these handy," said Resus, patting his cloak affectionately as he jabbed the burning torch in the wolf's face. Skipstone growled and pulled back.

Luke dashed around the desk to help Cleo to her feet. "How do we stop this thing?" he asked.

"That's the question we ask ourselves every time *you* transform," retorted Cleo.

54

Keeping the wolf at bay with one hand, Resus slid a pair of gardening shears from the folds of his cape with the other and tossed them onto the desk with a clatter. "I'll keep the werewolf occupied here," he shouted. "You sneak around behind him and snip off one of his claws!"

Luke stared at the shears. "You want me to cut off Mr. Skipstone's finger?"

"How else do you suppose we get it?" asked Resus, giving a sudden stab with the torch as the wolf tried to run along the edge of the room and escape. "If we wait for him to change back, it won't be a werewolf's claw anymore!"

Luke reached for the shears, then quickly pulled his hand away. "I . . . I didn't know I'd have to . . . None of the other relics had to be collected like this!"

"I agree," said Cleo. "We had to search quite hard for some of them. This one's right in front of us."

"No, I'm talking about having to hurt Mr. Skipstone to get it!"

"Then let me do it," she exclaimed, snatching up the shears.

Luke took them from her and sighed deeply.

"No," he said firmly, "it should be me. This is for *my* mom and dad—"

The werewolf gave a sudden roar and darted forward, jaws snapping and saliva spraying. Cleo squealed. "Well, go on and do it before we have to send you back to your world in pieces!"

Grasping the handles of the shears tightly, Luke slid around to the far side of the room, out of the werewolf's line of sight. Cleo jumped up and down behind Resus to create a distraction.

Once behind the wolf, Luke crept forward, the shears shaking in his trembling hands. Ducking to avoid the creature's furiously lashing tail and closing his eyes tightly, he slid the parted blades around one of its front paws—and slammed them shut.

When the expected scream of agony never came, Luke opened his eyes to discover the tip of one of the werewolf's talons on the floor before him. "Nice going, numb-nuggets!" shouted Resus. "You were supposed to cut off a claw, not trim his nails for him."

"He moved!" retorted Luke, then clamped his hand over his mouth as he realized he'd given away his position. The werewolf spun in a flash

 56

and leaped toward him, fangs glistening with hot saliva. Luke fell backward and the wolf advanced until it stood right over him. He pushed hard against its throat to keep the snapping teeth at bay.

Resus raced across the room toward his friend and leaped onto the werewolf's back. Furious, it spun around, launching the young vampire across the room and into the desk. The flaming torch fell from his hands and onto the aged M. T. Graves manuscript, setting it alight.

As Resus tried frantically to put out the flames, Luke's hand scrabbled across the carpet and grasped the largest book he could find. Swinging it up with all the force he could muster, Luke smashed it into the wolf's face.

The werewolf crashed to the ground, stunned. Luke struggled to catch his breath for a moment, then yelled, "Let's get out of here!"

The trio dragged the unconscious werewolf out into the garden of 1 Scream Street and collapsed, exhausted. Luke pressed his face into the cool grass and struggled to slow his pounding heart. Beside him, the silver werewolf growled deep in

its throat as the first waves of consciousness began to return.

Still breathing hard, Resus grabbed the shears from Cleo and pushed them toward Luke. "Do it," he said.

Taking them, Luke carefully placed the blades around one of the claws on the werewolf's left front paw. He looked away and then snapped them shut. The werewolf gave a semi-conscious whimper, and Cleo pulled a strip of bandage from her waist to stem the flow of blood.

As Luke picked up the werewolf's claw, the creature itself began to shrink in size. "I think Mr. Skipstone's coming back to us."

"The problem is, the book's gone," said Resus. "The manuscript of *Bandages of Doom* that we were going to use to hold his spirit—it went up in flames."

Luke sat up suddenly. "There's a copy of the book in my bedroom!" he exclaimed. "We can use that."

Just then, a hand burst through the lawn, quickly followed by the diseased green head of Doug, one of Scream Street's resident zombies. "Dudes!" he proclaimed. "What's the scoop?"

"Perfect timing," said Cleo. She helped Doug out of his tunnel and led him over to the now human but barely conscious figure of Samuel Skipstone, lying on the grass, his hand bloodied and bandaged. "Doug, could you please take Mr. Skipstone to my house?" she asked. "My dad will look after him until we get back."

"No problemo, little lady!" said Doug, lifting Skipstone into his arms and lurching unsteadily out of the garden.

Luke squeezed the author's good hand as he was carried away. "Stay with us, Mr. Skipstone," he pleaded. "I'll be with you as soon as I've got the book."

As the trio raced away toward Luke's house, Resus turned and called over his shoulder to the zombie, "If he wakes up, Doug, whatever you do — don't make him angry!"

# Chapter Seven
# The Doorway

**Luke, Resus, and Cleo** rushed back into Luke's bedroom, just as—"ACHOO!"—a bright orange flash transformed Luke's duvet into a roll of striped wallpaper.

"I see that Tress is still suffering with her flu," said Resus.

Luke slid the golden casket from under his bed and opened it to check that the relics were still OK. He sighed with relief when he saw that they were. "We can send her a get-well card once we've found an M. T. Graves book for Mr. Skipstone," he said, dropping the werewolf's claw in with the other founding fathers' gifts.

"Which box did you put the Horror Heights books into?" asked Cleo, rummaging through a collection of computer games.

"I think most of them are in these," replied Luke, opening up one of the ones by the wardrobe. As he did so—"ACHOO!"—another flash filled it with teddy bears.

"We'd better find them quickly before Tress's sneezes zap them into something unusable," said Resus. "I doubt we can transfer Mr. Skipstone's spirit into a cuddly pajama case!" He, Luke, and Cleo grabbed a box each and began to rifle through in search of a Horror Heights book.

Luke lifted a handful of CDs out of his box and found himself looking at a familiar image: the terrifying vampire on the cover of *Fangs of Destiny*. "Got one!" he shouted triumphantly, snatching up the book. As Resus and Cleo turned to see, the trio were suddenly bathed in a rainbow of light.

"What's Tress changed *now*?" demanded Cleo, shielding her eyes.

"This one doesn't seem quite the same. . . ." said Resus.

Hanging over the casket of relics was a shimmering, rainbow-colored archway. As Luke approached it, shielding his eyes with one hand, he began to make out a room on the other side.

"My bedroom!" he whispered.

"Top marks, werebrain—we're *in* your bedroom," quipped Resus.

"No, you don't understand," said Luke, stepping closer. "I mean *that's* my bedroom, on the other side—my *old* bedroom!"

Cleo stared up at the shimmering arch. "This must be your doorway home!" she exclaimed.

"What?" gasped Resus. "Why did you open it *now*?"

"I didn't," protested Luke. "I just dropped—"

He stopped. "I dropped the werewolf's claw into the casket with the other relics. . . ."

"And putting them all together must have activated the magic!" finished Cleo.

Luke held his trembling fingers out toward the shimmering entrance to his old bedroom. His old

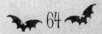

room, in his old house. He'd done it. The first person ever to open a doorway out of Scream Street.

He took a step toward the glimmering portal,

but Cleo grabbed his shoulder and held him back. "What are you doing?" she asked. "You can't go through now!"

"Mr. Skipstone said that the doorway would remain open until my greatest wish was fulfilled," Luke reminded her. "So as long as I don't take my mom and dad through, it should stay open." He stared through the arch into the world he'd often thought he'd never see again. "I just want to make sure it's real," he said, and taking a deep breath, he stepped through.

There was a brief moment of disorientation in which Luke was forced to close his eyes against the dizziness. For a second he didn't want to open them again in case the doorway was nothing more than a mirage. What if the founding fathers' relics *showed* you what you really wanted but stopped short of actually giving it to you? He didn't think he'd—

*Beep!* A car horn outside made him jump.

A car horn? But there were no cars in Scream Street. Slowly, Luke opened his eyes to find himself standing in the bedroom of his old house. The room was bare, as all the furniture had been moved with his family—but it was definitely his

own room. Luke ran his fingers over the familiar felt-tip marks he'd scribbled onto the wallpaper when he was little, and reveled at the sound of traffic in the street outside. He was home.

Turning back to the doorway, he could see Resus and Cleo standing just a few yards away in his Scream Street bedroom. Their mouths moved as they spoke, but their voices sounded muffled and distant. Between them and him, the golden casket lay open, the relics of the founding fathers pulsing with the same light as that of the doorway.

Luke tucked the Horror Heights book into his pocket and pushed his head back through the shimmering arch. The sounds of Scream Street quickly replaced those of his own world.

". . . long are you planning on staying there?" finished Resus.

"The relics worked," Luke said, beaming. "It's a doorway back to my world! Come and have a look!"

"What about Mr. Skipstone?" asked Cleo. "We have to get that book to him."

"Your dad's looking after him," said Luke, "and this will only take a minute or two. It could be the only chance you get to see where I'm from!"

Resus grinned. "I thought you'd never ask." He bounded through the portal and, after shaking his head to clear the dizziness, held his hand back through to Cleo. "Come on!" he called, his voice muffled.

Gripping his fingers tightly, Cleo allowed herself to be pulled through the shimmering doorway—and immediately crashed to the floor.

Luke helped her to stand. "The dizziness will wear off in a second," he said.

Resus gazed around the empty bedroom. "Well, this isn't exactly the brave new universe I was expecting," he said, a little disappointed. "It just looks like a bedroom."

"That's because it *is* a bedroom, clever-cape," Luke said with a grin. "Mine!" He hurried over to the window. "Look!" he shouted excitedly. "You can see the supermarket from here, and the park where I used to play football!"

Cleo joined him at the window just as a bus thundered by outside. The mummy screamed and ducked down, her hands over her ears.

Luke stared at her. "What's that all about?"

"Get down," hissed Cleo, grabbing a handful

of his T-shirt and pulling hard. "I think that was a dragon!"

Luke tried hard not to laugh. "Don't be silly," he said, "it was a bus!"

"I don't care what they call dragons in your world," snapped Cleo, "but wherever you're from, when a big green thing roars past, you hide!"

"Cleo, there were people inside it."

"And we'll be next if it spots us, you idiot," Cleo wailed, still tugging persistently at his shirt.

With a sigh, Luke crouched down next to his friend. "It's just the same as the tour bus that came to Scream Str—"

He was interrupted by a shout from down-stairs. "Luke, quick!"

Luke and Cleo ran down the stairs to find Resus in the hallway, staring at the front door. The letterbox rattled as the postman dropped a handful of junk mail onto the pile that had built up on the doormat.

"The front door's throwing up!" exclaimed the vampire, pulling a long silver sword from his cape. "It's probably not a real door at all—more likely to be a shapeshifter." He waved the sword threateningly. "Come on, coward, show us your true form!"

Luke placed his hand on Resus's arm and lowered the sword. "I don't think that bringing you two here was a very good idea," he said, grinning. "Come on, let's get back to Scream Street and Mr. Skipstone."

Cleo led the way back upstairs, with Resus guarding the rear in case the shapeshifter attacked. Luke looked contentedly around his bedroom. "Just think," he said with a smile, "I'll probably be sleeping in here again tonight."

"We'll miss you," said Cleo.

"I'm not going just yet," Luke reassured her, pulling *Fangs of Destiny* from his pocket. "First we've got some magic to do back in Scream Street!" He took a step toward the shimmering doorway.

"ACHOO!"

Just as Luke reached the portal, a muffled sneeze rang out from the other side. At his feet the golden casket was suddenly lit up by a burst of orange—and the vampire's fang was changed

into a pair of spectacles. The entire doorway exploded in a rainbow of colors, knocking Luke, Resus, and Cleo to the floor.

Luke jumped up and stared around the bare bedroom in disbelief. "No!" he shouted. "NO!" He ran his hands over the walls, trying to find a crack in the plaster that could be the portal back to Scream Street, but they remained smooth and solid.

"What was that?" demanded Cleo.

"Another of Tress's sneezes!" said Resus. "It changed the vampire's fang." He paled even further beneath his white face paint. "Without all six relics providing their magic, the doorway closed."

"We can open it again, though, can't we?" asked Cleo. "We can still get back to Scream Street?"

Her question was met with silence. Luke rested his forehead against the bedroom wall. "No," he replied quietly. "We're trapped here."

# Chapter Eight

# The Plan

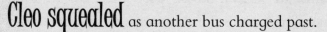

**Cleo squealed** as another bus charged past.

"If you're going to panic every time we're near a busy road, this will take forever," grumbled Luke, pressing the button for the pedestrian crossing outside the supermarket. It was good to see the familiar landmarks around his home again, but he couldn't stop worrying about what was happening back in Scream Street.

Despite Resus's and Cleo's protests, Luke had decided that if they were going to find another way back to Scream Street, that would mean going outside.

"I don't feel right," muttered Resus.

"Well, you *look* right, and that's what matters for now," said Luke. He had insisted that Resus remove his false fangs and wash off his white face paint before they left the house. The vampire now trudged along moodily, his cape folded up and stuffed into a plastic grocery bag.

"I wish you could say the same for me," grunted Cleo. "I don't look right at all, do I!" A disguise for the mummy had been a bigger problem, but luckily the Movers had missed one of Luke's parents' closets when relocating the family to Scream Street. Cleo was now wearing one of his mom's floral summer dresses, and a net curtain torn from the window of the downstairs bathroom covered her head as a makeshift scarf. "I look like an idiot," she moaned as the trio crossed the road. "I can't believe I'm wearing a *dress*!"

"Cleo," hissed Luke as they reached the other side, "if you walked around in my world wrapped from head to toe in bandages, you'd look as though you'd had a major accident and be carted off to the nearest hospital!"

"What about my face?" sulked the mummy. "The dress doesn't cover my face, and neither does this headscarf thing."

"If anyone asks, we'll say you've had an allergic reaction."

"What to?" asked Resus.

"It doesn't matter what to!" Luke yelled in exasperation. He took a deep breath and lowered his voice again. "It's just an excuse in case we need it." They had now reached the park, and Luke slumped onto a bench. His friends sat beside him.

"So," said Resus cautiously, "what's the plan?"

"I don't have a plan," admitted Luke. "Having spent all my time finding a way out of Scream Street, I never thought I'd need to break back in!"

"Eefa was at your house earlier," said Cleo. "The one in Scream Street, I mean. She was fixing the things that Tress had changed with her sneezes. Maybe she'll come back and do the same for the vampire's fang."

"I've thought of that," said Luke, "but she wouldn't know what she was looking for. No one knows we've been collecting the relics except the three of us."

"And Samuel Skipstone," added Resus.

Luke buried his face in his hands. "That's the other thing," he wailed. "Mr. Skipstone wasn't looking good when we left. If we don't get the Horror Heights book to him, he could die. In fact, he could already be—"

"Let's not think like that," Cleo interrupted hurriedly. "We have to stay optimistic and hope for the best."

"If only we'd told our parents that we were collecting the relics," Luke groaned. "At least then there'd be a chance of someone working out where we were and trying to help us get back."

"Actually, there *is* someone else who knows we've got them," said Resus. "Sir Otto Sneer." It was true. Ever since they had begun their quest, Scream Street's landlord had tried to steal the founding fathers' relics for himself so that he could use their power to further torment the "freaks" he despised so much.

"If we could somehow get a message to him," Resus continued, "he could show Eefa which of the relics has changed."

"And then walk off with them all?" retorted Cleo. "We can't let Sneer know where they're hidden after all we've been through."

"If it gets us back to Scream Street we might have to," admitted Luke. Sir Otto had created poltergeists, disabled the vampires' blood supply, and even created a demon in order to get hold of the relics. Now, leading him to them could be their only hope of returning to their families.

"We won't be able to contact him, though," said Resus glumly. "The only way to do that would be through G.H.O.U.L., and I doubt it even advertises its existence to people in this world, let alone its address."

Luke sat up. "Say that again!"

"What? That G.H.O.U.L. doesn't advertise its address?"

"No," said Luke excitedly, "the bit about getting in touch with Sir Otto through G.H.O.U.L.! It must be in contact with him somehow—it could help us get a message through!"

"That's an idea," agreed Cleo, "but Resus is right—I don't think that Government Housing of Unusual Life-forms will be common knowledge in this world. *You'd* never heard of it until the night you were moved. We'll never find them."

"Maybe we don't have to find them," said Luke, a smile spreading across his face. "How about we let them find us?"

"That's him," Luke said, pointing.

Resus pulled his cape back on and peered around the bush to get a better view. "*That's* the school bully?" he asked. "He doesn't look very tough to me." The trio was hiding across the road from Luke's old school, watching as the pupils went home for the day.

"There *is* something different about him," admitted Luke. "He'd normally be tripping the other kids by now, and calling them names—but he seems to be keeping to himself."

They watched as the bully fidgeted nervously with his tie, his eyes darting back and forth as he clung to the shadows.

"I guess that's what being attacked by a werewolf does to you," said Cleo.

Luke felt a twinge of guilt as he thought back to the moment he had transformed into a werewolf and attacked Steven Black. The bully had stolen the backpack of a younger girl, and as Luke had attempted to retrieve it for her, Steven had pushed him to the ground. A few minutes later, the bully had been running for his life as a werewolf pursued him across the adjoining church graveyard.

"Maybe it shouldn't be him," said Luke. "I think I've scared him enough for one lifetime."

"You're not backing out, are you?" asked Resus.

"Of course not," replied Luke. "But if I'm going to transform and attract the attention of G.H.O.U.L., I want to make as little impact as possible. Steven Black looks as though he's ready to snap!"

"OK," agreed Resus. "Let's choose someone else. . . ."

"We'll have to be quick," said Cleo. "There's only one kid left: that boy over there with the funny ear."

Luke looked to where she was pointing. "He'll do," he said. "Let's go!"

Scrambling out of the bush, the trio approached the lone boy. His left earlobe was torn, as though he'd been in an accident, and he instantly covered it with his hand in front of the strangers.

Luke cleared his throat. "I'm, er, very sorry to have to do this. . . ." He closed his eyes in concentration and began to summon the anger that would kick-start his werewolf transformation.

"I wouldn't do that if I were you, Luke Watson," said the schoolboy, and there was a

sound like running water as the child began to change shape, his body growing and stretching until, eventually, in his place stood a tall man in a long black leather coat and mirrored sunglasses.

The figure flashed a silver badge at the trio. "Zeal Chillchase, Tracker for G.H.O.U.L.," he said in a deep voice. "You three are under arrest!"

# Chapter Nine
# The Interrogation

**"I will ask you one more time!"** yelled Zeal Chillchase, slamming his hands down on the table in front of him. "What were you planning to do with that child?"

The trio faced Zeal across a table in a bare, windowless room. Luke gripped the sides of his chair and struggled to contain his temper. The

Tracker was trying to sound as threatening as possible, and Luke was determined not to give him the satisfaction of seeing him get angry.

"I've told you," he said wearily. "We just wanted to frighten someone so that G.H.O.U.L. would know we were here." On either side of him, Resus and Cleo nodded their agreement.

Chillchase glared at Luke from behind his mirrored shades. "You escaped from Scream Street, then came here just so you could get caught again? I find that *very* difficult to believe."

"It's the truth!" protested Cleo. "We didn't mean to get trapped here—the doorway closed accidentally."

Zeal leaned in toward the trio. "And how did you open this doorway?"

"We used the relics of Scream Street's founding fathers," explained Resus. "We've been helping Luke to collect them."

"So your plan to come here and attack a child was arranged in advance?"

"We didn't plan to attack anyone!" shouted Luke. "I just wanted to take my parents home."

Cleo touched his arm gently. "Calm down," she said. "If you get too angry—"

"Nothing will happen," finished Zeal. "This room — in fact, the whole of G.H.O.U.L. headquarters — is magically sealed against un-authorized transformations. Our vampire friend here will also discover that his cape has been deactivated." Resus quickly pushed his hand into his cloak to check and found nothing more than the silky blue lining.

"So, is that where we are?" asked Cleo. "G.H.O.U.L. headquarters?" After their arrest, Zeal Chillchase had opened a Hex Hatch — a kind of window in the air — that had brought them directly to this bare, lifeless room.

"Don't try the innocent act with me," Zeal replied. "I've been a Tracker long enough to have seen every trick in the book!"

"But we *are* innocent," insisted Resus. "The doorway opened before we expected it to. Luke was just showing us his old house when one of the relics changed and the doorway closed behind us."

Zeal ran his fingers through his hair. "The 'relics' again," he grunted. "There's no mention of any relics in *The G.H.O.U.L. Guide.*"

"*The G.H.O.U.L. Guide?*" asked Luke. "What's that?"

Chillchase reached into one of the pockets of his leather coat and produced a thick gold-covered book. He tossed it onto the table  with a thump. "A complete reference to every G.H.O.U.L. community in existence—and beyond," he said. "With no mention of any founding fathers' relics."

"There *must* be," insisted Luke, flipping open the book and skimming through its pages. "We can't be the first people ever to—"

He stopped, staring at the page in front of him. "I know that handwriting. . . . This was written by Samuel Skipstone!"

"That's right," agreed Zeal, surprised. "He wrote this for internal use here at G.H.O.U.L." He watched as Luke found the chapter on Scream Street and began to search for any mention of the relics. "How do you know about Samuel Skipstone?"

"He gave us clues to the locations of the

relics," said Resus. "That's it!" he exclaimed as a thought occurred to him. "You can ask Samuel Skipstone! He's being looked after right now by Cleo's dad, at twenty-two Scream Street!"

"Impossible," scoffed Zeal. "Skipstone died long ago, while working on his history of Scream Street."

"He merged his spirit with that book," explained Luke. "He lived on! That's how we know his handwriting."

"And you can show me the finished book, with Skipstone inside, as proof?"

"Actually, no," admitted Cleo. "It turned to ash after we brought his body back to life."

"You brought him back to life?" Zeal Chillchase exclaimed. "This gets more fantastical by the second! You should have planned your story a little better, children. Do you have any witnesses to back up your tale of these so-called relics?"

"Just one," said Luke. "Sir Otto Sneer."

"The landlord of Scream Street knows about the relics?"

Luke nodded. "Ask him."

Chillchase looked at him for a moment, then opened the door and beckoned to a Mover in a white jumpsuit who stood waiting outside. The Tracker pressed his fingers to the forehead of the faceless man for a second, who then nodded and hurried away. "If, by some chance, Sir Otto confirms your story, I've ordered for him to confiscate the relics."

"You can't let Sneer have them!" protested Resus.

"*If* they exist—which I doubt," retorted Chillchase, "they are important G.H.O.U.L. artifacts and should be kept safely by someone responsible."

"*Responsible?*" Cleo said with a snort. "I don't think we're talking about the same Sir Otto."

"We are," said Zeal. "He has a nephew, Dixon, who is a shapeshifter like me."

"So *that's* how you did the schoolboy trick!" exclaimed Resus.

"It helps in my work as a Tracker."

"You keep using that word," said Cleo. "What's a Tracker?"

"I find and observe unusual life-forms," explained Chillchase. "Then I pass their details on to the Movers, who relocate them to a G.H.O.U.L. community."

 85

"Is that what happened to me?" asked Luke. "A Tracker found me?"

Zeal paused for a moment. "I did," he said quietly.

*"You?"* demanded Luke, standing up so fast that his chair skidded across the room. *"You're* the one who condemned my parents to life in Scream Street?"

"I had no choice," barked Chillchase. "Your werewolf was dangerous, and it was only a matter of time before it seriously hurt or even killed someone!"

"I would never have done that."

"Oh, no?" said the Tracker. "Let's see, shall we?" Pulling a crystal ball from another pocket in his coat, he placed it in the center of the table and waved his hand over its surface. An image began to form inside the globe.

Resus and Cleo leaned in to watch as the school bully, Steven Black, was chased across the graveyard by Luke's werewolf. The creature pushed the terrified boy to the ground and was preparing to pounce, when a chihuahua leaped from the bushes, nipping the wolf in the leg. With a roar, the werewolf turned from the bully and went after the tiny dog instead.

Luke forced himself to watch the scene from behind his friends. "You were there!" he cried. "You looked on as I attacked Steven Black!"

"Better than that," replied Chillchase, pocketing the crystal ball. "I saved him." And he pulled back his hair to reveal the same damaged ear they had seen on the schoolboy.

"No," whispered Luke as he began to recognize the injury. "It can't be true. . . ."

"What's the matter, Luke?" asked Cleo. "What's he talking about?"

Zeal smiled. "Allow me to demonstrate." Taking a deep breath, the Tracker began to shrink. His leather coat became soft white fur and his arms transformed into tiny front legs. Within seconds, a chihuahua stood in front of the trio.

Resus stared at the tiny dog's scarred ear. "You're Fluffy!" he exclaimed. "The dog that stopped Luke from attacking the bully. He thought it was just a lucky coincidence, but you were following him!"

Zeal Chillchase shapeshifted back to his human form. "I tracked Luke right from the night of his first transformation," he revealed. "I was the ambulance driver who took him to the hospital on his tenth birthday, and a month later I watched as a spider outside his room while his parents tied him to his bed during the second attack."

He strode over to where Luke was standing, white faced. "You never stood a chance of get-ting away from me, Watson. None of your family ever does!"

"My family?" said Luke. "What are you—"

Suddenly the door opened and the Mover in the white jumpsuit entered. Once again, Zeal pressed his fingertips against the man's forehead for a second, then the Mover left.

Chillchase turned back to the trio. "Sir Otto Sneer says he knows nothing about any relics," he said.

Resus leaped to his feet. "That's a lie!" he

shouted. "He's been trying to get them from us ever since we met Samuel Skipstone!"

The Tracker continued. "He did, however, send details of how, ever since Luke moved to Scream Street, the three of you have worked to make the lives of your fellow residents a misery."

*"What?"* said Cleo indignantly.

"You infected your neighbors with vampire Energy," recited the Tracker, "you also released a swarm of suffocating spiders, took an unauthorized trip to the Underlands, and even built a demon from the body of the Headless Horseman!"

"We had to do those things to stop Sir Otto," insisted Luke.

Chillchase snarled. "Who do you think I'm going to believe? The respected landlord of a G.H.O.U.L. community, or three kids I caught selecting an innocent schoolboy for an unprovoked werewolf attack?" And with this he opened the door again to admit three more Movers, this time dressed in black jumpsuits. They each grabbed one of the children and handcuffed their wrists behind their backs.

Zeal Chillchase removed his sunglasses for the first time and glared down at the trio. "Luke

Watson, Resus Negative, Cleo Farr . . . I hereby sentence you to be moved to separate G.H.O.U.L. communities for the remainder of your natural—or unnatural—ives."

Cleo's eyes flooded with tears as she struggled against her bonds. "Where are you sending us?" she asked, her voice cracking.

Chillchase replaced his sunglasses with an air of finality. "Anywhere but Scream Street!"

# Chapter Ten

# The Escape

**Luke rested his head** against the cold bars of the door to the holding cell and watched as Movers in jumpsuits of varying colors carried full body bags past them and off along the corridor. "This is all my fault," he groaned.

"This is all my fault," repeated a troll from the corner of the cell.

Resus threw the monster a look and joined his friend. "How is it your fault?"

"I got you involved in the hunt for the relics in the first place," said Luke. "If I'd gone looking for them on my own, we wouldn't be in this position."

"Wouldn't be in this position," said the troll.

Cleo stood up from where she had been squashed on a bench between a sleeping banshee and a drunken gargoyle and glared at the troll. "Do you mind?" she snapped. "This is a private conversation!" She hurried over to Luke. "If it wasn't for our help, you'd still be looking for the first relic," she said.

"She's not wrong!" Resus said with a grin.

"And," continued Cleo, "over the past few weeks we've had the best adventures of our lives! We wouldn't have missed them for the world."

Luke gave a faint smile. "It's just a shame it all has to end this way."

"All has to end this way." The troll's rumbling voice echoed around the cell.

Before anyone could say anything, the door to the cell was yanked open, and Zeal Chillchase appeared. Without giving the children so much

as a glance, he read aloud from a piece of paper in his hand, "Lan Mossdrop!"

A small man with the head of a wasp stepped out of the shadows at the back of the cell. "No," he gurgled. "You can't do this to me!"

A Mover stepped out from behind Zeal and grabbed Lan Mossdrop, dragging him out of the room and over to a wooden platform on the far side of the corridor.

"For invading a nursery school and using the human toddlers as bowling pins, I sentence you to life in the Underlands!" announced Chillchase.

The wasp creature began to scream as the Tracker pulled hard on a nearby lever. A trapdoor set into the platform opened beneath Lan Mossdrop, and he fell into the blackness below.

"At least we haven't been banished to the Underlands," said Luke with a shiver when Zeal left. "I don't like the look of that trapdoor!"

"I don't like the look of that trapdoor!"

Ignoring the troll, Cleo watched as another group of Movers went past, carrying more colored body bags, each with a still figure inside. "What are they?"

"They're how you're moved to your new G.H.O.U.L. home," explained Luke, remembering the evening he had watched his parents being zipped into similar bags by the Movers. "I guess the purple ones are destined for Scream Street."

"They'll probably split us up among the other colors," sighed Resus.

"I hope I don't get green," said Cleo, struggling not to cry. "It doesn't suit me!"

Luke stared unhappily at his friends. "I'm so sorry."

"I'm so sorry," repeated the troll.

Luke turned angrily to where the monster was sitting. "All right," he demanded, "why are you doing this?"

"Doing what?" rumbled the troll.

"Repeating everything I say," barked Luke. "It's really annoying!"

"It's really annoying," moaned the troll.

"There!" said Resus. "You're doing it again. Why?"

The troll shrugged its boulderlike shoulders. "You are sad. I want to be sad too. I don't know how."

"You don't know how to be sad?" asked Cleo.

"I've heard that about trolls," Resus said. "They don't feel emotions in the same way as we do. They have to learn them."

"Is that why you're copying us?" asked Luke. "You're learning how to be sad?" The troll nodded.

"Why do you *want* to be sad?" said Cleo.

"Lan—the wasp man—went to the Underlands," replied the troll flatly. "I cannot go. They are sending me somewhere else. He is my friend."

"They're moving you to a separate location from your friend?" said Luke. "We know what that feels like."

"That is why I copy you," the troll said, sniffing. "I want to feel it too." It turned to Cleo. "You understand. You are part troll."

"Sorry," said Cleo, "I'm not a troll at all. I'm a mummy."

"But you have a troll arm," replied the monster, tapping her plaster cast clumsily.

"That's just lotus flower," Cleo said with a laugh. She ran her fingers thoughtfully over the tough cast for a second. "What's your name?" she asked.

"Wompom," said the troll.

Cleo grinned. "Well, Wompom, you might just have given me an idea."

"I TOLD YOU TO STOP COPYING EVERY-THING I SAY!" roared Luke.

Wompom the troll climbed to its feet, its head bent to stop it from scraping the ceiling of the cell. "I WILL SAY WHAT I WANT!" the monster bellowed.

"I warn you—I'm in enough trouble not to

96

care what I do!" screamed Luke, beating at the troll's chest with his fists. "They can't punish me any more than they are already!" Other creatures began to back away from the fight that was erupting in the middle of the cell.

"You can do nothing to me," growled Wompom. "I will squash you." The troll grabbed the bench, unseating the still-sleeping banshee, and swung it at Luke's head. Luke ducked and the bench smashed against the metal bars of the cell.

"That's it," hissed Resus. "Keep it up. . . ."

Luke grabbed a piece of the broken seat and rattled it along the bars. "Come on," he taunted. "Come and do your worst!"

The Mover on guard quickly unlocked the door to the cell and entered just as Cleo leaped out from behind it. She dealt him a blow across the back of the head with her plaster cast, and the Mover fell to the floor, unconscious.

"I told you these things were tough," said Cleo, grinning.

Luke gestured toward the open cell door. "Quick," he urged. "Before they notice."

Wompom patted him on the head with a rough-skinned hand. "You *have* taught me a new feeling today. The feeling of trusting some-one new." Then the troll lurched out of the cell and hurried over to the trapdoor that led to the Underlands.

Cleo found the lever and pulled hard. With a creak, the trapdoor opened beneath Wompom's feet and the giant creature fell through. As the wooden hatch swung back into place, the troll could be heard shouting below, "I'm coming, wasp man. . . ."

"Right," said Luke, turning back to Resus and Cleo. "Let's go!"

The trio raced along the bare corridor, passing a number of closed doors as they went. Each room

had its department name written on the door: Fang Licensing, Homes for Gnomes, Apparition Chamber. Nothing, however, looked as though it might be a holding room for body bags.

As they turned the corner, Luke, Resus, and Cleo suddenly found themselves face-to-face with another leather-coat-wearing Tracker, dragging a handcuffed skeleton along beside him. "Yuri Pinetop," said the Tracker, eyeing the children suspiciously. "I'm taking this fugitive to the holding cell."

"Trumpton Bakedbeans," announced Luke, saying the first thing that came into his head. "These two are being taken to identify fellow criminals."

"Why aren't you in official Tracker uniform?" asked Yuri.

"The mummy hit me with a spell," Luke lied as convincingly as he could. "It caused my shapeshifting muscles to stick in child form. Once these two identify their accomplices, they're going straight to the Underlands!"

"A member of staff in the Apparition Chamber should sort out your shapeshifting," said Yuri as he began to lead the skeleton away.

"Er . . . the spell affected my memory, too," Luke called after him. "Where are the body bags kept again?"

"Second-to-last door on the right," yelled the Tracker over his shoulder.

"Thanks!" Luke called back, then he noticed Resus's amused expression. "What?" he said defensively. "I found out where the body bags are, didn't I?"

"You certainly did, *Trumpton*!" the vampire said with a grin.

Before Luke could retort, an alarm suddenly sounded.

"They must be on to us!" cried Luke, and he, Resus, and Cleo dashed back along the corridor. They pushed open the door marked Outgoing Life-forms, where occupied body bags in a rainbow of colors were piled from floor to ceiling.

"You know what to do," Luke said to the other two. "Just make sure you choose purple!"

Quickly unzipping one of the bags, Luke found himself looking at the scaly yellow body of some kind of snake with a human face. "Can I hitch a ride?" he whispered to the unconscious creature, slipping in beside it and pulling the zipper closed.

 100

Seconds later, the door crashed open. "They're not in here!" called a voice. "Keep searching, they can't have gone far."

Luke froze beside his unwitting companion, breathing as shallowly as he could and hoping that Resus and Cleo had had similar success.

"Get these bodies onto the trucks," ordered another voice. Luke felt his bag being lifted up and carried away, and the sound of the alarm faded fast.

The last thing he heard was the angry voice of Zeal Chillchase echoing along the corridor. "I'll find you, Luke Watson. Wherever you go—I'll find you!"

# Chapter Eleven
# The Decision

**Luke waited** until he heard the last of the Movers leave the house, then he unzipped the body bag and slipped out from beside the still-unconscious snake creature. The plan had worked: he had been moved back to Scream Street, along with its new residents. "Thanks for the ride," he quipped before stepping out onto the landing to discover Resus and Cleo emerging from other bedrooms. "You made it!"

"Of course," said Resus, smiling. "I *adder* great journey."

"Come on," said Luke with a groan. "We've got to get to Mr. Skipstone."

The trio left the house and began to run in the direction of 22 Scream Street, stopping suddenly when they spotted Niles Farr marching across the central square, a limp figure under each arm. As they hurried over, the towering mummy carefully laid Samuel Skipstone and an unconscious Sir Otto Sneer on the ground.

"Dad!" exclaimed Cleo. "What's going on?"

"You were a long time," said her father. "Mr. Skipstone was worried."

The author looked pale and weak. He coughed as he tried to sit up, but then slumped back down with the effort. "You were gone so long," he wheezed, wiping his forehead with his bandaged hand, "that I knew something was amiss. I came to find you and discovered Sir Otto with these . . ." He opened his jacket to reveal a golden casket decorated with hieroglyphics.

"The relics!" cried Cleo. "Sneer found them!"

"I knew he'd search my house as soon as G.H.O.U.L. told him where we were," said Luke. "He was probably going to take them back to Sneer Hall while he found a way to restore the vampire's fang."

"And my dad knocked him for a loop!" said Cleo proudly.

Niles Farr bowed slightly. "It was a pleasure to do so."

"There they are," called a voice across the square. Luke turned to see his own parents racing toward them. Resus's mom and dad were just a few steps behind.

Mrs. Watson threw her arms around her son. "Where have you *been*?"

"You wouldn't believe me if I told you," smiled Luke. "But I thought I'd left you behind!"

"You look different," Alston Negative said to his own son.

"I'm working under cover," replied Resus. "Oh, hang on . . ." He reached into the folds of his cloak and produced his false fangs. "Hey, my cape's working again!" he beamed, clipping them into place.

Just then, the door to Everwell's Emporium

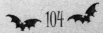

opened and Eefa Everwell dashed out. "They're back!" she called to Tress Wunder, who came running out behind her.

"And they're safe," spluttered Skipstone, collapsing into another coughing fit. As he fumbled in his jacket pocket for a handkerchief, a piece of paper dropped out onto the ground. Mrs. Watson snatched it up to stop it from blowing away.

"It's not *us* we need to worry about, but *you*," said Luke, leaving his parents and kneeling beside the frail old man. "Resus, can you still remember the spell?"

*"Rats live on no evil star,"* announced the vampire, joining him.

"Good," said Luke, reaching into his back pocket. "Now we just need a pen, and then we can—"

He froze. "The M. T. Graves book . . . It's gone!"

"It can't be," said Cleo, frantically checking Luke's empty pockets. "We need it!"

Luke shook his head. "It must have slipped out when I was in the body bag."

"Or when you were pretending to fight

Wompom," groaned Resus. "It could be anywhere!"

"The other Horror Heights books will still be in your room," said Cleo, jumping to her feet. "I'll go and get one!"

Samuel Skipstone shook his head slowly. "There is no time," he said sadly. "I am afraid this is good-bye."

"It can't end like this," cried Luke in frustration. "We came back to save you!"

"You *have* saved me." The author smiled fondly up at him. "I now know that my work has been of value. It has helped someone I care for very much! It was a joy to meet you, Luke Watson."

And with one final breath, Samuel Skipstone lay back and closed his eyes.

Luke's own eyes flooded with tears. "It's not fair!" he shouted. "All we needed was one of your books!"

"Try this one," said a voice behind him. A heavy golden book thudded to the ground beside Luke: *The G.H.O.U.L. Guide.* He looked up to see Zeal Chillchase standing over him. "I said I'd find you."

"What are you going to do?" asked Luke fearfully.

"I'm going to watch you save Samuel Skipstone," replied Chillchase.

Deciding he simply had to trust the Tracker, Luke quickly reached into Skipstone's jacket and found an old, roughly hewn pencil. "I need some paper," he said.

"Here," said Mrs. Watson, handing over the piece that had dropped from Skipstone's pocket.

Resting it on the author's chest, Luke carefully wrote out the spell: *Rats . . . live . . . on . . . no . . . evil . . . star.*

For a moment nothing happened, then a wisp of silver light rose from Skipstone's mouth and hovered for a moment before dashing into the pages of *The G.H.O.U.L. Guide.* The book vibrated slightly, then a golden face began slowly to appear on the cover.

Luke, Resus, and Cleo all held their breath. Had the spell really worked? Slowly, the author's eyes opened and he looked around. "I seem to have put on a little weight," observed Samuel Skipstone.

"Yes!" exclaimed Luke, hugging Cleo and giving Resus a high five. Everyone around them cheered. "We did it!"

"Amazing!" said Mrs. Watson, taking the pencil and paper from her son before he poked someone's eye out with it.

With a soft hiss, Samuel Skipstone's body gave a small shudder, then dissolved into ash. "And only just in time," said Resus. "But what do we do about these?" he added as the breeze stirred the ashes and threatened to scatter them.

"I have just the thing," said Tress Wunder,

producing one of her silver quill boxes and gathering up Skipstone's remains into it. "Perfect!"

Clutching *The G.H.O.U.L. Guide* to his chest, Luke stood to face Chillchase. "Now I suppose you have to take us to our new homes," he said.

"Hang on a minute," interrupted Mr. Watson before Zeal could reply. "I've seen some strange things since I've lived in this street — most of them in the past two minutes! — but no one is taking my son anywhere. He hasn't done anything wrong."

"Actually, Dad, I have," said Luke. "I've been collecting relics from Scream Street to find a way out of here for you and Mom, but I went too far and tried to scare someone with my werewolf. Mr. Chillchase was right to stop me."

"You've been trying to find a way home?" asked his mom.

Luke nodded. "I nearly did it, too. We were so close."

"Just minutes away, in fact," added Resus, stepping up beside his friend.

"I'm sorry, Luke," said Cleo, joining them. "Even though we found all six relics, it was all for nothing."

"Are these the relics you tried to tell me

about?" asked Zeal Chillchase, crouching to open the golden casket and examine the objects inside.

"They most certainly are," replied Samuel Skipstone, his golden face smiling out from its new home. "A werewolf's claw, the blood of a witch, a mummy's heart, flesh from a zombie, a skeleton's skull, and . . ." He paused, scanning the ground. "There should be a vampire's fang there too, but that appears to be missing."

"It's there," said Luke, indicating the spectacles. "It just needs a little magical attention."

"To think you three did all that to try to help us!" said Mrs. Watson proudly.

"So what happens now, Mr. Chillchase?" asked Alston Negative.

"Are you taking our children?" demanded Niles Farr.

"G.H.O.U.L. has ordered for them to be moved to new locations," said the Tracker flatly. "However, that cannot be arranged if I am unable to find them."

"You mean we can stay in Scream Street?" exclaimed Cleo.

"I haven't seen you—or these so-called relics," announced Chillchase with a faint trace of a smile. "So I guess there is nothing I can do." He grabbed the still-unconscious figure of Sir Otto and slung him over his shoulder. "Your landlord and I, however, *do* have a lot to discuss!" And with that he marched away toward the gates of Sneer Hall.

"Meanwhile, back to the relics," said Luke. "Eefa, could you change these glasses back to their original form, please?"

Tress Wunder stepped forward. "Allow me," she said. "I'm feeling much better now, and it's the least I can do after all the trouble I've caused!" She waved her hand over the pair of spectacles, and in a final burst of orange light, they changed back into a vampire's fang.

Instantly, the doorway sprang into life again, and there was a murmur of surprise among the adults. Luke's world shimmered into life beyond

the rainbow of colors, and Mr. Watson peered cautiously through the arch. "What's that?" he asked.

Luke grinned, handing *The G.H.O.U.L. Guide* to Resus. "It's our old street," he said. "The doorway has opened just in front of our house."

Luke's mom peered through the lights to see her home just yards away. "You mean it's . . ."

"A way out of Scream Street," Luke finished. "And I'm not waiting for anything to go wrong this time!" He turned to Resus and Cleo. "Thank you for everything." The trio hugged.

"I will not cry," Cleo muttered under her breath. "I will *not* cry."

"Suit yourself," laughed Resus, tears running down his own cheeks. "I'm just glad Luke made me wash off my face paint!"

Luke stepped away from his friends and took one final look around him at Scream Street. "Come on," he said to his mom and dad. "Let's go home." He started toward the glowing doorway.

"No," said Mrs. Watson.

Luke stopped. "No?" he asked. "Why?"

"We *are* home, Luke," replied his mom. "Look at you: you've got friends, you're helping people . . .

 113

you're happy! That's what *I* call home."

"But . . . You're terrified here!" insisted Luke.

"We're getting used to it—slowly," said his dad. "Besides, I don't look forward to going back to my old job. It's no life, spending every minute working. I get to spend much more time with my family here." He winked at Alston Negative. "Even if the neighbors *are* a bit odd!" The vampire bared his fangs with a smile, and Mr. Watson pulled back comically. As he did so, he knocked the piece of paper from his wife's hand.

"What's this?" asked Luke, picking it up and beginning to read.

"Er, you just wrote the spell on it two minutes ago," said Resus. "It came from Mr. Skipstone's pocket. Don't tell me you really have got shape-shifting brain freeze!"

"I don't mean that," said Luke. "I mean this headline . . ."

Cleo peered over his shoulder to read aloud, "*'Announcing the wedding of Arran Skipton to . . .'*" She stopped. "Arran Skipton?"

"My son," explained Samuel Skipstone. "I told you he dropped a few letters from our surname to protect his family from being traced by

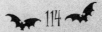

114

G.H.O.U.L. Skipstone became Skipton."

"But my mom's name before she got married was Skipton," said Luke. His eyes widened and he stared at the author's golden face. "You don't mean . . . ?"

Samuel Skipstone nodded. "Now that you've decided to stay, I can reveal everything. *You're* my family, Luke. My great-great-great-great-great-great-grandson, if you want to be precise."

Cleo stared, open-mouthed.

"Wicked!" Resus said with a grin.

Luke felt a lump in his throat. Thoughts of his old life evaporated like a rapidly fading dream. Scream Street was where his family belonged—where *he* belonged. He smiled up at his parents. "You OK?" he asked.

"I'd say we're more than OK," said his mom. "Who knew we had a famous author in the family?"

"This calls for a celebration," said his dad. "Let's go to thirteen Scream Street!"

Luke took the silver box containing Samuel Skipstone's ashes from Tress Wunder and turned to Resus and Cleo. "Yes," he smiled. "Let's go *home*."

## Chapter Twelve
# The Problem

**Steven Black hurried** to school through the park, jumping at every noise and shadow. He was certain he'd spotted Luke Watson the night before, watching him from the bushes, but he hadn't seen him since.

Forcing away the memory, he made his way over the crosswalk outside the supermarket and took the shortcut along the road where Luke and his family had once lived. The Watsons had disappeared shortly after the werewolf had—

"Stop it!" he told himself sternly. "It wasn't real. It didn't happen. As the doctors and therapists have all said, it was just a bad dream!" But the dryness in his throat remained.

As he reached Luke's old house, he noticed a slight shimmer in the air beside him. In fact, now that he looked, there appeared to be some kind of rainbow-colored doorway hovering over the pavement. Through it he could see tall, mis-shapen houses and some kind of shop in the center of a square.

All thoughts of school forgotten, the bully stepped through the arch. . . .

**Tommy Donbavand** was born and raised in Liverpool and has held a variety of jobs, including clown, actor, theater producer, children's entertainer, drama teacher, storyteller, and writer. His nonfiction books for children and their parents, *Boredom Busters* and *Quick Fixes for Bored Kids*, have helped him to become a regular guest on radio stations around the U.K. He also writes for a number of magazines, including *Creative Steps* and Scholastic's *Junior Education*.

Tommy sees the Scream Street series as what might have resulted had Stephen King been the author of *Scooby-Doo*. "Writing *Scream Street* is fangtastic fun," he says. "I just have to be careful not to scare myself too much!" Tommy lives in England with his family and sees sleep as a waste of good writing time.

You can find out more about Tommy and his books at his website: www.tommydonbavand.com